Who's running Dawn's life?

"Okay, try to make a basket, Dawn," said Terri, shooting her the ball.

Dawn stood on a crack in the driveway (the free throw line) and threw as hard as she could. The ball bounced off the rim of the basket but did not go in.

The girls looked at each other meaningfully.

"Well, you were close," said Sonya.

"I think you'll be better at track," said Terri.

"What's all this track stuff?" Dawn asked.

"Hey, that's a great idea, Dawn," said Angela.

"Yeah. You should be in track, you're so fast," said Jennifer.

"If I was in seventh grade, I'd do it," said Monique.

"I never run," said Dawn.

"You run after your little brother," Angela pointed out.

"That's different," Dawn replied.

"Look, why don't you sign up for track tomorrow?" suggested Sonya.

"Well, I—" Dawn began.

Terri cut her off. "It's too late. I already signed you up."

"You did what?" asked Dawn in horror.

Books by Susan Smith

Samantha Slade #1: Samantha Slade: Monster Sitter
Samantha Slade #2: Confessions of a Teenage Frog
Samantha Slade #3: Our Friend: Public Nuisance #1
Samantha Slade #4: The Terrors of Rock and Roll

Available from ARCHWAY Paperbacks

Best Friends #1: Sonya Begonia and the Eleventh Birthday Blues
Best Friends #2: Angela and the King-Size Crusade
Best Friends #3: Dawn Selby, Super Sleuth
Best Friends #4: Terri the Great
Best Friends #5: Sonya and the Chain Letter Gang
Best Friends #6: Angela and the Greatest Guy in the World
Best Friends #7: One Hundred Thousand Dollar Dawn
Best Friends #8: The Terrible Terri Rumors
Best Friends #9: Linda and the Little White Lies
Best Friends #10: Sonya and the Haunting of Room 16A
Best Friends #11: Angela and the Great Book Battle
Best Friends #12: Dynamite Dawn vs. Terrific Terri

Available from MINSTREL Books

#12 Dynamite Dawn vs. Terrific Terri

by

Susan Smith

A MINSTREL® BOOK

PUBLISHED BY POCKET BOOKS

New York   London   Toronto   Sydney   Tokyo   Singapore

A MINSTREL PAPERBACK *ORIGINAL*

 A Minstrel Book published by
POCKET BOOKS, a division of Simon & Schuster
1230 Avenue of the Americas, New York, NY 10020

ISBN: 0-671-72487-8

First Minstrel Books printing February 1991

10 9 8 7 6 5 4 3 2 1

For Michael

Dynamite Dawn vs.
Terrific Terri

Chapter One

❀

"Dawn, come down from there! It's not going to work," called Linda Carmichael, one of Dawn Selby's best friends.

Dawn was hanging by her arms from a tree in Linda's backyard. She was trying to stretch herself to make herself taller. Her friends Linda, Angela King, Sonya Plummer, Jennifer Soo, and Monique Whitney stood watching.

Just then another of the girls' friends, Terri Rivera, appeared. "What's she doing?" Terri asked the others, scratching her spiky dark hair.

"Hanging from a tree," supplied Sonya.

"Thanks for telling me," said Terri. "I wouldn't have known."

"She's trying to stretch herself to make herself taller," Angela explained.

"So that maybe, just maybe, I can play basketball next year," said Dawn.

"Dawn, the only thing you're going to do is get arms like a monkey's," warned Sonya.

"And they don't allow monkeys on basketball teams," said Jennifer.

"Most likely you'll pull your arms out of their sockets," added Linda. She twisted her long blond ponytail into a corkscrew.

"Give it up," said Terri. "Shrimps don't make basketball players."

Dawn let go of the tree and fell to the ground, her fine blond hair flopping across her eyes. "Okay, okay. I'll stop."

"Where's the ball?" asked Terri. Linda tossed her a basketball. "Want to throw a few hoops?"

"Sure." Dawn was the first up and dribbled the ball into the driveway, where the basketball hoop was hung above the garage.

Terri stole the ball from her, and Dawn ran to recapture it. She got in front of Terri and bounced the ball away, but instantly lost control of it. The ball rolled into the street, and Dawn chased after it. She stopped it before it reached the gutter on the far side.

When she rejoined the others, Terri said, "You're pretty fast, you know. You're going to enjoy track."

"What?" asked Dawn, dumbfounded.

"I'll tell you about it later," Terri said, snatching the ball from Dawn's hands and passing it to Linda. "Let's play."

Linda dribbled the ball twice and went in for a perfect layup. As the ball went through the hoop, everyone cheered and yelled, "Swish."

"What do you mean, I'm going to enjoy track?" Dawn asked Terri, getting the rebound and circling away from Terri with her back to her.

"Yeah. Do you mean she's going to enjoy watching you run, Terri?" asked Monique.

All the girls knew how much Terri was looking forward to

track season at their new school, Banner Junior High. Sonya, Dawn, Linda, Angela, and Terri were in seventh grade. Monique and Jennifer were in sixth, and still went to Gladstone Elementary.

"I said I'd tell you later," said Terri, reaching around Dawn and stealing the ball. Terri was the most athletic one in the group.

"I can't stand the suspense, Terri. What're you saying?" Dawn asked, desperately trying to guard Terri, who faked a jump shot and then raced around her and up to the basket to pop the ball in.

"You'll find out soon enough," Terri said mysteriously, getting her own rebound and passing to Sonya. Sonya shot from ten feet out. Dawn tried to jump and block the ball, but her arms weren't long enough and she only tripped and fell over her own feet.

"What a champ!" teased Linda, grabbing the rebound.

Monique and Jennifer, who were also short, had just as much trouble with the game as Dawn and yelled at Linda to stop it.

Dawn jumped and tried to bat the ball out of Linda's hands. She got a hand on it but couldn't control it, and the ball rolled straight toward Linda's house.

"Oh, no! It's going under the porch!" cried Dawn, taking off after it.

Dawn dove for the ball, but it disappeared under the porch before she could get it. She slid on her hands and knees a good ten feet.

Her friends gathered around to help her up.

"Well, there's one thing being short is good for," said Angela.

Dawn stared up at her friend, whose dark curly hair framed her pretty, round face. "What's that?"

"You can crawl under porches easily," Angela told her.

Dawn stared at the dark crawl space. "You've got to be kidding."

"Nope. I can't fit in there," said Angela, sticking her arms out to demonstrate.

"Neither can I," added Linda.

"The only thing tall people think short people are good for is doing the dirty work," said Jennifer. She was Chinese-American and had pulled her long black hair into two pony-tails that day.

"Well, we are good at getting into tight spots," Monique agreed. She was tinier than Dawn, black and extremely skinny.

Terri stuck her hands on her hips. "Okay, you guys. Let's not argue. I thought we were going to play ball. You knocked the ball, you get it."

Impatiently, she tugged on Dawn, yanking her closer to the crawl space under the porch.

Dawn knelt in the soft dirt and peered into the darkness of the crawl space. She wrinkled her nose. "It smells funny," she said, inching forward.

"Go!" ordered Terri, nudging her from behind.

Dawn flattened herself, then began crawling. The ground felt cold and wet under her hands. As she moved, she could feel cobwebs cling to her face. Reaching up to pull them off, she shuddered and looked around for the ball. Finally she saw it outlined by a thin stream of sunlight filtering in through the floorboards above her.

She put her hand back down to crawl for it and touched

something furry. "Aaah!" she screamed and tossed her head back, knocking it on the floor above. "Ouch!" The something furry skittered out from under her fingers.

"What's wrong?" cried six voices outside. They sounded so far away!

"There's something alive under here!" Dawn yelled back.

"Any snakes?" Sonya asked worriedly.

"My brother found one under there once," said Linda.

Dawn felt a cold shiver run up and down her back. "I'm coming out!"

"No. Get the ball first," said Terri fiercely.

"I don't want to," Dawn whimpered.

"You have to!" Terri insisted.

Dawn crawled backward until her bottom stuck out into the breeze. She felt a pair of hands suddenly shove her back in. She thumped forward onto her chin. "Ugh!"

"You're not coming out empty-handed," said Terri.

"But I'm scared," said Dawn.

"Don't be a wimp," Terri ordered.

"I bet *you* wouldn't want to be under there," Sonya pointed out.

"Yeah," said Linda.

"That's not the point," said Terri. "She knocked the ball—she gets it."

"All right. All right, I'll do it!" Swallowing her fear, Dawn crawled toward the ball as quickly as possible. Reaching it, she turned around and gave the ball a little shove until it rolled out into the daylight. Dawn quickly followed.

Her friends' faces filled the opening as she scrambled out.

"Are you okay?" they asked all at once.

"Wow, you smell funny," said Jennifer, pinching her nose shut.

"It stinks under there," said Dawn, pulling at cobwebs and wiping dirt off herself. "I never want to do that again."

Linda dragged a piece of plywood over to cover the opening. "There. Now you won't have to."

"What a heroine!" cried Angela, swatting at Dawn to help her dust herself off.

"Can we please play ball?" asked Terri, twirling the basketball on her index fingernail, the way she'd seen a pro ball player demonstrate.

Back on the driveway, Terri began dribbling the ball, under her legs, behind her back, and around her body. Dawn tried to guard her, but Terri's arms were longer and she managed to stay away from Dawn.

"Face it, basketball is not your sport," said Terri.

"But I want to play more than anything," protested Dawn.

"You have to know your limitations," Linda said. "Look at me. I can't do a lot of things you can do."

"Like what? Climb under your house?" asked Dawn.

"Well—I can't wear children's shoes," Linda offered.

"Yeah. They don't cost as much," said Monique.

"But you're probably too tall for elevator shoes," giggled Sonya, tugging at the waist of her new shiny neon-purple shorts. She was the most fashion conscious of the group.

"And I can't get into the movies for half price," Linda said.

"I'd rather pay full price," said Dawn.

"All the boys are taller than you," said Angela.

"Big deal," Dawn said. "I don't care about boys anyway."

"Okay, here, make a basket, Dawn," said Terri, passing her the ball.

Dawn stood on a crack in the driveway that the girls used as the free-throw line and tossed as hard as she could. The ball bounced off the rim of the basket, but didn't go in.

The girls exchanged a meaningful glance.

"Well, you were close," said Sonya encouragingly.

"You'll be better at track," said Terri.

"What's all this about track?" Dawn asked.

"That's a great idea, Dawn," said Angela.

"Yeah. You should sign up for track, you're so fast," said Jennifer.

"If I was in seventh grade, I'd do it in a minute," said Monique.

"I can't run," said Dawn.

"Of course you can. You run after your little brother all the time," Angela pointed out.

"That's different," Dawn replied.

"Why don't you just sign up? They're having the last day of sign-ups tomorrow," suggested Sonya.

"Well, I—" Dawn began.

Terri cut her off. "It's too late. I already signed you up."

"You did what?" asked Dawn in horror.

Chapter Two

❀

Dawn stood staring at Terri with her mouth hanging open. Just then a boy from their class at school, Lyle Kraus, cruised by on his bike. Dawn cringed. Lyle had a major crush on her, and she knew he was checking up on her.

"Hey, I understand you signed up for track, Dawn," he said and rode on, weaving a little as he waved back at her.

Dawn gasped, then whirled around to glare at Terri. "You did it! You really did it!" she exclaimed. "Why?"

"Because I knew you were upset about not being on the basketball team," Terri said, grinning. "So I thought track would be great for you."

"You could've asked me first," Dawn said. "Don't you think I should have something to say about it?"

"You would've said no, but don't worry—you'll be great. Track tryouts are Monday, but the first thing we have to do is get you some track shoes," said Terri. "We'll go after school tomorrow. And I'll coach you. There's hardly anything to learn."

Dawn nodded. "I just love it when my friends make my

decisions for me." She had almost forgotten that she was guilty of doing that same thing herself.

"Okay, let's start working right here and now," said Terri, pulling Dawn out to the sidewalk. She pointed down the street. "From here to the end of the block is about one hundred meters." Terri glanced at her sports watch. "Ready, set, go!"

Dawn stared at her in confusion. Terri gave her a push.

"Go, Dawn. I said, go, G-O!"

The next day at school, Thursday, Dawn, Terri, Angela, Linda, and Sonya were in their homeroom class just before the first bell rang.

The teacher, Mrs. Bender, walked over and spoke to the girls. "I'm glad to see you girls signed up for the environmental club," she said to them. Her voice was twittery, like a bird's.

"Huh?" said Terri, blinking in confusion.

"What environmental club?" asked Sonya.

"Yeah, what environmental club?" asked Linda.

"Shhh," warned Dawn in a whisper. "Don't say anything in front of the teacher."

"But what's she talking about?" Terri wanted to know.

"I'll tell you after class," hissed Dawn.

"I'm so impressed with these five girls," Mrs. Bender announced to everyone in the room. "They've joined the environmental club, Save a Tree. For anyone else who's interested, see Mr. Walinsky." The bell rang soon after that.

Terri zoomed out of the room and waited for Dawn in the hallway. The other girls gathered around them.

"Okay, what's this about a Save a Tree club?" Terri demanded.

"Well, I signed you up. All of you," Dawn told them. "I thought it would be good for us."

"What?" they gasped in unison.

"You did this just because I signed you up for track!" declared Terri hotly.

"No, I didn't. I just thought it would be a nice thing to do."

"Nice for who?" Terri asked.

"Whom," Sonya corrected.

"Nice for all of us," replied Dawn. "Something we could do together."

"We'll have track," Terri said.

"You know that's not what I mean," Dawn said, becoming exasperated. "Track doesn't help Earth Month."

"Well, maybe, but I still think you did this on purpose just because of what I did," said Terri.

"No, I didn't. Anyway, I had signed us up before then," Dawn admitted.

All the girls gasped. "What?" they cried again.

"What was all that about checking with people first before making a decision for them?" Linda asked.

"Yeah, you sure were mad at Terri about that yesterday," Sonya pointed out.

"Well, this is different," Dawn said.

"How is it different?" Terri asked.

"I was sure you guys would want to do something for the good of the earth," Dawn told them.

They were quiet for a moment. Then Sonya said, "I think it's a great idea."

Dawn gave her a grateful look.

"Yeah, it does sound nice," said Angela.

"Uh-huh," Linda agreed.

"Well, what's it about?" Terri asked.

"They'll tell us at the first meeting at lunch today," said Dawn.

"Any more surprises?" asked Terri.

"Look who's talking," said Dawn.

At lunch the group gathered in one of the English classrooms for the Save a Tree Club meeting. Mr. Walinsky, club advisor, Howard Tarter, Eddie Martin, Lyle Kraus, and a new boy, Ryan Wilcox, were the only seventh graders there.

"You didn't tell me Ryan Wilcox was in this club," Terri whispered to Dawn.

"I didn't know," Dawn replied. She watched Terri watching Ryan. He was tall and walked a little stooped over, but he had thick curly brown hair and nice brown eyes.

"We want to know what this club is about," Linda announced.

"Since someone signed us up for it," added Angela, giving Dawn a sidelong glance.

"It was for your own good, I'm sure," said Howard. "Saving a tree never hurt anybody."

"The club was formed to do something useful for Earth Month," explained Mr. Walinsky. "We won't just save trees, we'll plant them, recycle bottles, cans, and paper, and in general work to clean up our environment. This weekend we're planning to plant trees."

"It'll be up near Sonya's ranch," added Lyle.

"Anyone interested?" Howard asked.

Terri's hand shot up in the air. All the other kids raised their hands, too.

"I'll ask my mom and stepdad if we can have a cookout afterward," said Sonya.

"Now that sounds good," said Lyle.

"We'll also need someone to put together a poster or something for the display case in the front hall at school," said Howard.

"I'll do it!" Dawn shouted. She was glad to see that her friends were interested.

"See? What did I tell you," she said to them afterward.

After school the five girls rode their bikes to the Gladstone Mall. Terri led the way into the sports shop and told the saleswoman that Dawn needed track shoes.

"You will be fitted better in a child's shoe," said the saleswoman, after measuring Dawn's feet.

They trooped over to the children's section, where they found striped, spotted, and neon-bright sneakers.

"Too bad you can't get track shoes with Minnie Mouse on the toes," said Terri.

"Very funny," said Dawn.

Dawn was fitted with shoes that had cleats on the bottom. "They feel funny," she said.

"You'll get used to them," said Terri. "The cleats will help your feet grip the track."

The girls then strolled into Sundaze, their favorite ice-cream parlor, and ordered sundaes.

"There's Ryan Wilcox," announced Terri, looking out the window and nodding toward the fountain in the center of the mall.

"He's cute," said Angela.

"He's also really shy," said Terri. "He never says a word."

After school the next day Dawn and Terri were the first ones out on the track to practice. Dawn wore a pair of pink shorts, a T-shirt, and her new track shoes. Terri explained that she had to time Dawn at different distances.

"We'll start with the shortest distance," she said. "A hundred meters is up to that first post." She pointed to a post next to the track.

"How do you know so much about this?" asked Dawn.

"I've watched the Olympics, and I've read about it," Terri replied. "Now for short dashes, the starter will say 'Take your marks.' That's when you put your knee on the ground and your other foot on the starting line, your hands on either side of your front foot. That's right. When I say 'Get set,' you lift your behind, and when I say 'Go,' you go. Now stand on the line and I'll time you."

Dawn did as she was told. When Terri yelled "Go!" Dawn took off from the starting point as fast as she could. She heard the wind whistling in her ears and her feet thudding underneath her. She liked the sounds and the way it felt to run. Within seconds it seemed, she was at the finish line.

Terri ran up to her. "You did really well! Gosh, you're fast, Dawn."

"Thanks."

"Make sure you don't run pigeon-toed, though," Terri said.

"Do I?" Dawn asked worriedly.

"Well, just a little. Just try not to do it again."

"Okay. Let me go again." Terri timed her once more. This time Dawn was very aware of her feet.

"Much better, but you'd better stop eating doughnuts for breakfast," Terri said.

"No doughnuts?" Dawn asked. Her parents owned a bakery in town.

"Right. You have to keep up your strength by eating only good foods if you're going to be in track," said Terri.

Dawn wasn't sure about this, but she decided Terri must know what she was talking about. "I guess I can eat bran muffins," she said.

"Or cereal," said Terri. "And you need a lot of sleep."

"Try getting sleep in my house," said Dawn. She had two rowdy brothers and two sisters living at home. When she looked at Terri, she noticed her friend wasn't paying any attention to her. Terri's attention was riveted on the outdoor swimming pool, where Ryan Wilcox was standing close to the chain-link fence, toweling off. He was on the school swim team, which had an after-school practice.

"Terri, do you like Ryan or something?" asked Dawn.

"Like him? What do you mean? I like him okay," Terri said, pacing back and forth. "But he's just a guy."

"But what about Tommy? Is he just a guy, too?" asked Dawn.

"Tommy and I are friends," Terri insisted. "Anyway, he's in Mexico on vacation for a while."

Dawn sighed. Terri had been insisting Tommy was just her friend for over a year now. But if Tommy so much as looked at another girl, Terri became madly jealous.

"Well, I hope Tommy doesn't get jealous," said Dawn, studying Terri's face.

Terri pretended to ignore her. She watched Ryan as he disappeared into the boys' locker room.

Dawn giggled. She thought all this boy-girl stuff was funny. She wasn't at all interested in boys, but her friends were.

"So that's why you wanted to coach me in track today. You knew Ryan had swim practice," she told Terri.

"It is not," Terri insisted, but Dawn knew how Terri liked to keep her feelings hidden. She'd never in a million years admit she liked a boy.

Friday before school Dawn was in the hall, putting up a display in the front cabinet. Her display consisted of a globe and several posters with photos of polluted city air, a nuclear waste dump, trees dying in a park, and birds trapped in an oil spill. Opposite them she put up photos of kids recycling cans and glass, planting trees, turning off lights to conserve energy, and helping animals at a nature refuge. The main caption read: EARTH MONTH—SAVE OUR PLANET!

She was reaching up, trying to push a thumbtack into the top of the cabinet. She had wrapped a string around the thumbtack and tied the globe to it.

"Need a hand?" asked a voice behind her.

She turned around and saw Ryan standing there.

"Oh, sure. Thanks," she said. "I've always wanted to be tall. But I'm not."

"Well, we all come in different sizes and shapes," he said, easily sticking the thumbtack into the ceiling. "There. Anything else?"

"No, thanks. Everything else can be done by a short person," she told him. "Hey, how do you like the Save a Tree Club?"

"So far, so good," he told her.

"See you on Saturday, then," said Dawn.

"Yeah. See you." Ryan smiled and walked away.

Terri and the others joined Dawn just then. "I can't believe it," Terri exclaimed. "Ryan actually spoke to you."

"Well, sure. He helped me hang up my globe," said Dawn.

"For a moment he had the whole world in his hands," said Angela, and everyone laughed.

"Maybe I'll get to talk to him when we go tree planting," said Terri.

"What about Tommy?" asked Angela, who thought about romance almost all the time.

"What about him? He can't go with us because he's in Mexico with his parents," said Terri.

"Lucky guy. He gets out of school for a whole three weeks."

"But he has to write essays on everything he did," added Linda.

"Does he know you're interested in Ryan?" asked Sonya.

"It's none of his business. And who says I'm interested in Ryan?" said Terri.

"Who knows? He might meet somebody else in Mexico," said Linda, arching one eyebrow. She had traveled a lot. "It's a very romantic place."

Terri tried to look as if it didn't matter to her. "Who cares?" she said.

Dawn wrapped her arm around Terri. "Hey, no big deal. Terri and Tommy are just friends, guys," she told the others. They all giggled.

* * *

On Saturday Dawn and her friends, including Jennifer and Monique, met at Sonya's ranch for the tree-planting expedition. Howard Tarter, Lyle Kraus, Eddie Martin, and Ryan showed up too. None of the eighth graders in the club could come because they had a field trip scheduled.

The small California town of Gladstone, where the girls lived, was located between beach and mountains. Sonya's ranch was in the foothills, but not far from the center of town.

Sonya's mother, Nellie Stretch, had offered to chaperone the group because Mr. Walinsky had an emergency early that morning. Howard, an avid environmentalist, had brought along fertilizer and shovels for digging. He was helping Sonya's stepfather, Bob Stretch, load the supplies onto the wagonbed. About twelve spindly young trees lay in the wagonbed, their root balls swathed in burlap bags. Horses were saddled and tethered outside the barn.

Sonya gathered everyone together. "We're going to plant in an area of the forest that was damaged by fire. The holes have been partly dug—all we have to do is finish digging and plant."

"We should get extra credit at school for doing this," suggested Jennifer to Monique.

"I'd do it anyway," said Monique, gazing at the trees.

"Jen, put on a pair of my jeans," Sonya suggested. "You're going to get your clothes messed up." Jennifer was wearing a pink and purple jumpsuit, much too good for planting trees.

Jennifer went into the house and emerged a few minutes later wearing a pair of jeans that were far too big for her. Everyone laughed, and she complained.

"Come on," Sonya said, cinching the pants into gathers with a belt. "This is not a fashion show. Let's get going."

Almost everyone rode in the wagon, except for Terri, Sonya, and Dawn. They rode on horseback. Before Dawn could protest, Lyle jumped up behind her on Amigo.

"Don't put your arms around my waist," Dawn told him.

"But I might fall off," he said. "There's nothing else to hang on to."

"You can ride in the wagon," Dawn protested.

"Let him hang on to you," Sonya said, giggling as she rode by. "It'll be fun."

"Fun for who?" Dawn asked.

"Whom?" Sonya corrected.

The others giggled. Dawn cringed as Lyle wrapped his arms securely around her waist.

The riders followed Mr. Stretch up the trail. When they reached the bare patch of forest that needed planting, everyone helped unload the trees. Lyle followed Dawn everywhere.

She dragged a small tree over to a nice sunny spot where a hole had been started. Lyle decided to dig in the same hole opposite her. They bent over at the same time and bumped heads.

"Lyle, do you have to be right there?" she asked.

"Well, no, but I can't dig in the same hole if I'm somewhere else," he replied, grinning.

"Why don't you get some water from the creek?" she suggested, figuring that would keep him busy for a while.

He was gone for ten minutes. By then she had dug the hole big enough. He helped her build up a small mound in the bottom of the hole to set the roots around. Then he started to pour a little water on the root ball, but tripped and dumped the entire bucket on it.

"You're drowning it!" cried Dawn.

"Sorry. Just trying to help," he said, shoveling dirt into the hole.

Dawn was ready to lose her cool. "Don't touch the tree! Don't touch anything!"

Everyone turned to look at them.

"She's having a fit," said Lyle. "Look how nice our tree looks."

"It's lopsided," said Dawn. "It can't stand up in all that water."

Mr. Stretch came ambling over, looking amused. "Uh, Lyle, that tree looks like it's trying to take root in the Rio Grande."

Lyle looked at his handiwork and shook his head. "Well, I guess I'll have to shovel out some of this mud, then."

While Lyle shoveled, Dawn replaced the mud with dry dirt.

Dawn glanced at Terri and saw that she was watching Ryan, who was busy working with Howard. Dawn heard her ask, "How's it going?" Ryan smiled and said fine.

"Hey, Dawn, I think I've got most of the mud out," said Lyle.

She turned toward him just as he was flinging out the last shovelful of mud. He hit her square in the face with the squishy black mud.

"Oh, wow. I'm sorry," he said, dropping the shovel and running to her. "Here, let me help."

Gritty mud hung on Dawn's eyebrows, slowly oozing down her face. "Don't touch me," she warned.

Lyle looked confused and a little hurt. Mr. Stretch offered her a beach towel and a bucket of water to wash in.

"Hey, Dawn, it's just mud," said Lyle comfortingly.

"Yeah, I think mud is supposed to be good for your complexion," said Sonya.

The others laughed. Dawn, who almost never got angry, was ready to kill him.

Chapter Three

At Sonya's house Dawn took a shower and washed her hair before changing into some of Sonya's clothes. Then she joined the others for a cookout.

"Hey, we look like twins in our oversize clothes," commented Jennifer.

"I think you look kind of funky," said Howard.

Sonya's mother and Bob Stretch grilled hot dogs and hamburgers for the group. Then everyone took off on horseback to watch the sunset. They rode high up into the hills, and when they got to the top, Sonya and Howard dismounted and held hands. Terri had ridden next to Ryan most of the way and tried to make conversation. Finally, when she got tired of talking to herself, she cut back and rode next to Dawn.

"He doesn't say anything except yes or no," complained Terri. "I don't know why he won't talk to me."

"He's just shy," said Dawn. But she remembered he had talked to her with no trouble at all.

"Want to hold hands and watch the sunset?" asked Lyle, who reined up on Dawn's other side.

"Now here's someone who is not shy," said Dawn. "No thanks, Lyle."

As Dawn pulled her horse away from Lyle, Amigo kicked out toward Lyle's horse. His horse reared, then turned and bolted into the woods. "Help!" Lyle yelled.

Sonya heard him screaming and got to her feet. "What's wrong?"

"His horse took off that way." Dawn pointed.

Sonya jumped on Shadow and she and Dawn galloped off in search of Lyle. They could still hear him shouting "Help" far off in the distance.

Finally the yelling stopped, but they could hear splashing sounds. "Over here!" Lyle called. The girls rode in the direction of his voice.

Lyle was standing all alone in a stream, sopping wet. "I'm so glad you came. The horse sort of dropped me off here."

"Are you okay?" Dawn asked worriedly.

"Sure. I'm probably bruised, but I'll live," said Lyle.

"Sleepy is usually so quiet. I wonder what spooked him," said Sonya.

"That horse is named Sleepy? I can't believe it," said Lyle.

"Come on. Get up behind me," offered Dawn. Lyle hoisted himself up behind her quickly, before she changed her mind.

"Thank you for rescuing me," he whispered in her ear. She cringed.

On Monday, the day of the track tryouts, Dawn and Terri were on the track with thirty-five other kids. Dawn put on her new cleats and stomped around in them for a few minutes, while Terri stretched and warmed up. Angela, Sonya, Linda, Jennifer, and Monique sat in the bleachers, watching.

Soon Coach Mitchell gathered together all the girls who were trying out. "There's something for everyone in track and field," he said. "We just have to determine what you're good at. Usually, we use taller people in the longer races and shorter ones in the dashes. But we need many people to make up a track team, so we'll probably use all of you for something. First we're going to test how fast you run, and then we'll test you in the other events."

They lined up at the starting line and ran individually, while the coach clocked them. Dawn and Terri each ran the 100- and the 400-meter dash. Dawn got a good time in the 100-meter dash, but ran out of steam in the 400. Terri got the best time in the 400. After all the girls had run, Coach Mitchell called them together again.

"Okay, my best times were fourteen seconds flat for the hundred-meter dash. Those runners were Terri Rivera, Dawn Selby, Debbie Winston, and Gail Thornby. Those running at fifteen seconds were as follows . . ." He rattled off more names.

Dawn jumped up and down. "I'm so excited! Maybe I can be a runner after all."

Terri grinned. "See? I told you."

"Now, we're going to test for a few other events, such as the high jump and broad jump. Then I'll decide where to use each of you on the team."

The girls lined up once more for the next events. Dawn did well on the high jump, clearing four feet, eight inches on her third try.

"I'm surprised at you, Dawn," said Coach Mitchell. "It's unusual for a short person to do as well as you did on the high jump. Try the hurdles."

"You need long legs for the hurdles," Terri whispered knowingly.

"Who says? Coach Mitchell thinks I can do it," protested Dawn.

The hurdles were set up, and more girls lined up for the race. Dawn charged at the hurdles, knocking down the first three. But the coach was encouraging. "You have good technique. All it takes is practice."

When it was all over, almost everyone had been chosen for the team. Dawn decided not to do hurdles because she liked the high jump and running best.

Terri and Dawn passed close to the swimming pool on their way to the locker room.

"I think I'm going to love track," Dawn said enthusiastically.

Terri wasn't paying attention. She was checking out the boys, looking for Ryan. Just then he called out, "Hi, Dawn."

"Uh, hi," Dawn replied, turning deep red.

Once they were safely past the pool, Terri turned to glare at her.

"Why does he talk to you and not to me?" Terri asked. "I was walking right next to you, smiling at him."

"Maybe he thinks your name is Dawn and my name is Terri," suggested Dawn.

"Everybody knows my name," insisted Terri. "That's no excuse."

"But he's new here," Dawn said. "He might be confused."

"Maybe," said Terri.

Ryan's saying hi put a damper on Dawn's great day. She wished he wouldn't say anything to her, especially if it was going to make Terri angry. But she wondered why he spoke to her and not to Terri.

Chapter Four

❀

"The developers are coming!" declared Sonya, marching into Dawn's house the next Saturday.

"What's going on?" asked Dawn. She, Terri, Linda, Angela, Monique, and Jennifer were sitting in the kitchen, having cocoa and doughnuts. Dawn's seven-year-old sister, Tammy, was sitting with them, dribbling cocoa down her chin.

"Do you mean bust developers?" asked Jennifer.

Everyone burst into laughter.

"What're bust developers?" asked Tammy seriously.

"Something you don't have to worry about," said Dawn, giggling.

"What's so funny? I sent for one of those once," Jennifer replied.

Terri gazed at her chest. "Did you ask for your money back?"

"Very funny," said Jennifer.

"I'm talking about building developers," said Sonya, flouncing down in a chair. "They want to build condominiums up near our ranch. They're going to chop down trees and clear the land. The whole thing would be terrible for the environment.''

"I thought that was protected forest," said Terri.

"Not all of it," replied Sonya. "Some of it is privately owned, which means the owners can do anything they want with it, like sell it to developers.''

"Unless we can get the city to step in and say no," said Linda.

"We could write to our congresswoman and let her know about it,'' suggested Angela.

"Shouldn't we let the Save a Tree Club know?" asked Dawn.

"I think we should just stay here today and write letters,'' said Linda. "We can show the club what we've done on Monday.''

"Do you have a typewriter?" asked Monique.

"Yes, we do," said Dawn. "But it's down at our bakery.''

"Let's go, then," said Terri, starting for the door. Everyone scurried to gather up their things and follow her.

They rode their bikes down to the Fresh Bakery, where Mrs. Selby greeted them from behind the front counter.

"Well, how are you girls today?" she asked, smiling. Like her daughter, she was petite and blond.

"Fine," they chorused. Then Dawn explained that they needed to use the typewriter.

"Go right ahead. We hardly ever use it," said Mrs. Selby. "I hope it still works.''

They trooped through the kitchen, said "hi" to Mr. Selby, and located the typewriter in the small back office.

"Who can type?" asked Jennifer.

"I can," said Sonya. "I'm a reporter, remember?" Sonya sat down in front of the typewriter, while the others thought of things to say. They were going to write a letter to the city planning commission first.

"We have to make it peaceful," said Dawn. "We don't want them to think we're one of those groups that bomb people who don't agree with them."

"Or that we'll chain ourselves to trees in protest," said Angela.

"We're in the seventh grade," Sonya reminded them. "We would never think of doing that."

"We would if we got mad enough," said Linda, grinning.

They stared at Linda warily. "You have such a devious mind," said Dawn.

"I wouldn't do it, really, you guys. Don't worry," Linda said, laughing.

"Linda just likes to get you excited," said Jennifer.

The girls had to make several drafts of the letter before it was ready to go.

"We can send the same letter to our congresswoman and the city planning commission. All we have to do is change the name and address," said Dawn.

"Brilliant!" cried Terri.

"Do we write 'Dear Planning Commission'?" asked Dawn.

"No, silly," said Sonya. "My mom knows someone on the commission." She called and asked her mom the woman's name. "We address it to Dorothy Bidwell, and our congresswoman's name is Olga Crabtree."

The letter read as follows:

Dear _____:

We belong to a school group called the Save a Tree Club. It is our purpose to save trees and plant new ones. Trees provide our environment with oxygen, which we need more and more as our air gets dirtier and dirtier. Besides, trees add to the beauty of our land.

A group of developers is threatening to clear land in the mountains above Gladstone. They want to build condominiums. This land is valuable to our environment. We should leave it alone. We are the children who will have to live with this mess. Please stop the developers from ruining our forest land. Thank you.

The Save a Tree Club

After the letter was typed perfectly, each girl signed her name at the bottom. Monique and Jennifer, as unofficial members of the club, signed it, too.

"I just wish I was in junior high," lamented Jennifer. "I love to be in clubs."

"And I'd like to be on the track team," said Monique. "I love to run."

"Well, you can help with the Save a Tree Club," said Angela, holding her arms out wide. "Our club is big enough for the whole world!"

Jennifer licked doughnut sugar off her fingers and held the letter up to the light. "It looks great."

"Except for your sticky thumbprint in the corner," Sonya pointed out.

Sure enough, Jennifer had left a sugary, sticky print on the corner of the letter.

"Oh, no! I'm sorry," she cried, trying to rub it off.

"Just don't touch it anymore," said Dawn.

"Does this mean you have to type it over?" asked Jennifer.

"Maybe," said Sonya. "But we'll see what the rest of the club thinks of it first."

"Now it's a 'scratch and sniff' letter," said Monique, giggling.

"More like 'scratch and lick,' if you ask me," said Linda. "Why don't you just send our congresswoman a box of doughnuts?"

"That's not a bad idea," said Terri.

"I don't know about that," said Dawn worriedly. "It sounds like bribery to me."

"Yeah. Maybe we should just stick with our sticky letter," said Sonya.

Chapter Five

❀

"It sounds so professional," said Howard after reading the letter aloud at the Monday lunch meeting of the Save a Tree Club. "I think we should be asked to go to Washington to speak in front of the Senate."

"Hurrah!" everyone shouted, clapping wildly. The meeting was being held in Mr. Walinsky's classroom. Mr. Walinsky was the best kind of advisor—he sat back and let the students run their own meeting.

"First we have to get local attention," said Linda.

Ryan raised his hand. "Are people around here interested in ecology?" he asked.

"*Very* interested," said Terri in a loud voice. Then she stood up and smiled at him. "In fact, that's all anybody around here thinks about."

"No, it isn't," protested Eddie Martin. "There are a lot of people who want the developers in this town because they bring in extra money."

"Yeah. Extra people mean extra money," said Sonya.

"We may have to do more than write letters," said Ryan.

Everyone turned to look at him.

"Like what?" asked Terri.

"We may have to go on TV or the radio," said Ryan. "That's what my parents did when we lived in New Mexico."

"My mother is a filmmaker," Terri blurted out. "She has connections, especially when it comes to causes."

The bell rang. Everyone got up and started out the door. Terri and Dawn walked together to their next-period class, math.

Ryan, who was in their class, was already at his desk when they arrived.

"How'd he get here so fast?" Terri muttered under her breath.

"I can't imagine anyone getting here any faster than you," said Dawn, taking her seat two desks in front of Ryan.

He got out of his seat and walked up to Dawn's desk. "Oh, uh, Dawn. Do you have a pencil I can borrow?"

She glanced up at him, feeling embarrassed. From across the room she could feel Terri glaring at her. She dug around in her backpack until she found an extra pencil. "Sure, here's one," she said, handing it to him.

He smiled. "Thanks." Then he returned to his seat.

Dawn could feel Terri's eyes on her for the entire class period. When the bell rang, Terri instantly fell into step beside her.

"Well, you certainly talk to Ryan a lot," she said.

"Terri, that's not true. He talks to me," she said, then realized she'd stuck her foot in her mouth.

"You just want him for yourself," Terri accused. "Admit it."

"I don't! I don't even like boys," insisted Dawn. "I can't

stand the way Lyle follows me all over the place. I bet I won't *ever* like them!''

"There's always a first time, and I think this is it," said Terri.

"Terri! I'm a feminist," cried Dawn. "Besides, even if I *liked* boys, I wouldn't take one away from you." Terri didn't listen—she just walked away.

Dawn was upset. She didn't want to admit to Terri that deep down she was beginning to like having boys notice her. At least they weren't completely ignoring her anymore. She wondered if she could get interested in somebody just because he was interested in her. That wouldn't happen, she decided. Lyle was interested, and he drove her crazy.

After school Dawn and Terri met on the field outside for track practice. Coach Mitchell stood up in front of the group and began talking about what it was like to be in track.

Terri nudged Dawn in the side and whispered, "I heard he gives this speech before every track meet, so we'll have it memorized soon."

Dawn nodded and smiled, relieved that Terri was still speaking to her.

"Okay, some of you eighth-graders have already taken track before and know what it's about. But you seventh-graders, listen carefully. We will practice every day after school, five days a week. Our first meet will be two and a half weeks from today, so we've got a lot to do. We're going to practice every event that we'll enter in the meet. Everything you do will be timed. The relays are done in what we call 'split-time,' where we record each individual runner's time in addition to the total team time. Now today we'll practice the dashes, relays, and a couple of field events. Any questions?''

No one had any. Dawn followed Terri to the starting line for the 100-meter dash. Dawn ran as fast as she could, wind blowing her hair straight back and singing in her ears. Before she knew it, she crossed the finish line, just behind Terri.

''It's such a short race,'' she said to Terri afterward.

''Short, but sweet,'' Terri said. ''You did that in thirteen-five seconds.''

''Wow.'' Dawn was impressed with herself.

Next they practiced the relay. Four people would run a hundred meters each of the 400-meter relay. The first runner had a baton, which she passed on to the second runner, who would pass it to the third, and so on. The last runner, or anchor, had to be the fastest, because she would be the one to bring the team home.

Coach Mitchell placed Dawn at the beginning and Terri in the anchor position, because she was so fast. There was a twenty-meter zone in which to exchange the baton, and if the baton didn't get exchanged in that twenty meters, the whole team was disqualified. Dawn worried about this right up until Coach Mitchell said ''Go!''

Then she ran, clutching the baton. The next girl, Holly Weisenberg, was waiting with her arm outstretched. Dawn didn't let go of the baton until she was sure the girl had it firmly in her grasp. Once she had stopped, she watched Holly run and hand it off to Debbie Bryant, who fumbled and dropped the baton. She picked it up, stumbled, and ran on.

Terri was gazing off into space—probably thinking about Ryan, thought Dawn. When the baton reached her, however, she suddenly sprang to life, wrapped her hand around it and tore down the track toward the finish line.

"Go, Terri!" yelled Dawn, clapping her hands wildly.

Afterward, Coach Mitchell gathered the girls around him and read them their times. "Dawn, fourteen; Holly, fourteen; Debbie, sixteen; and Terri, thirteen-five. Very good first time out, girls."

"Wow, Terri, you were fast," said Dawn admiringly.

"Yeah, I was good, wasn't I? You were good, too, Dawn." Then Terri grinned at everyone. She loved being the best more than anyone Dawn knew.

Just then Lyle wandered over to where the girls were. "Hi," he said to Dawn. "I just wanted to let you know I saw you out there. You're fast. I didn't know you could run like that."

"Neither did I," admitted Dawn. "I always thought I was a slowpoke."

"Isn't it fun to find out you can do something you didn't know you could do?" Lyle asked.

"Well, I helped her get started," Terri butted in. "Of course, she is fast."

"Terri's the best teacher in the entire world," said Lyle admiringly. Terri had taught him how to fight once when he was being terrorized by bullies.

"Yes, she is. If it weren't for Terri, I wouldn't be able to put one foot in front of the other," said Dawn, smiling at her friend.

Terri grinned happily. "Well, you might be able to, but you also might trip."

Lyle laughed. "That's how I was when she taught me how to fight. I was all thumbs."

"And fists," added Dawn.

"You were just afraid," said Terri. "Most people are just afraid to do new things. They just have to try."

"That's right. I'm always afraid to try new things," Dawn admitted. "But I'm really glad you signed me up for track, Terri. This could be the best thing I ever did."

Chapter Six

❀

"Guess what?" Terri shouted as she screeched to a halt on her bike outside Dawn's house Tuesday morning. Dawn, Linda, Angela, and Sonya were there already, waiting for her, standing by their bicycles.

"What?" they chorused.

"My mother spoke to Mr. Walinsky, and she's arranging for us to be on cable TV to talk about Earth Month," Terri reported breathlessly.

"That's exciting," said Angela. "When?"

"Well, it will have to be soon because this is Earth Month," Linda pointed out, and pushed off on her bike.

"Brilliant deduction," Terri shouted after her, and pushed off, too.

"What will we say?" asked Dawn, pedaling as fast as she could to keep up with Terri.

"What will we wear?" asked Sonya, joining the line of her four friends on their bikes.

"We'll have to write a script or something. Find out more stuff about ecology," said Linda.

"Howard would be the best person to ask," said Angela.

"Howard even recycles the pop-tops off soda cans," said Sonya. "He knows everything about the environment."

When they arrived at school, the girls were excited and charged inside to locate Howard, who was next to the drinking fountain.

"To what do I owe this honor?" he asked, standing at attention. "All five of you want to talk to me at once. How lucky I am."

"We want to talk about ecology," said Sonya.

"About being on cable TV to talk about Earth Month," said Dawn.

"We want to know what we should do," said Angela, "Shall we write a script? Wear costumes?"

"Well, I've been wanting to wear a Smokey the Bear suit for a long time," said Howard thoughtfully.

"And I could be a tree with lots of healthy green leaves," added Dawn.

"Hey, guys, this shouldn't be the *Wizard of Oz,*" Linda said.

"We have to have a meeting," said Howard.

They decided the meeting had to be at lunch again because so many kids couldn't come after school.

At the meeting Mr. Walinsky explained how the show was going to work. He also told them that they would have to do research, which they could present on the air.

"I'll give each of you a script to memorize prior to the show," he said.

"Oh, no, I can't memorize," wailed Dawn. "I couldn't memorize the preamble to the Constitution."

"These will be only one-liners, Dawn," said Mr. Walinsky. "It won't be as hard as the preamble, believe me."

"And plus, we'll be talking about subjects we know about, like recycling," suggested Angela.

"And planting trees," added Linda.

"And land developers," Sonya said.

"And disposable diapers," put in Howard.

"Disposable diapers!" everyone chorused in surprise.

"Well, yes. They are a real problem and threat to our environment," Howard explained.

"I don't wear diapers, so I wouldn't know about it," said Eddie Martin. The group snickered.

"Howard has a good point. Disposable diapers are a problem," said Mr. Walinsky. "So are plastic grocery bags and aerosol sprays—many products that we just take for granted and use freely."

There was a lot to think about, thought Dawn. She hoped she wouldn't get confused, flub her lines, or burp in the middle of a sentence.

The next Saturday morning Dawn met her friends at the cable TV station, KIST, "the sun-kissed station." The five girls plus Howard, Eddie, Lyle, and Ryan sat in the green room—which was where the guests waited before going on—and worked on their lines.

"It's time to put on makeup," announced Sonya suddenly.

"I hope that doesn't apply to us," said Howard.

"Yeah, I think I'm beautiful enough without any," said Eddie, primping for the girls.

"So are the girls," said Ryan, batting his long silky eyelashes.

Terri grinned at him. "Yeah, we are, aren't we?"

"We just want to look extra glamorous for the camera," said Angela.

Finally, they disappeared into the dressing room.

"Ryan actually spoke," said Terri. "I think he has a sense of humor buried somewhere in that thick head."

"He doesn't have a thick head," said Dawn. "He's a nice guy."

"If he doesn't pay attention to Terri, he has a thick head," Angela said, defending her friend.

Sonya put an arm around Terri. "Terri, he loves you. He just can't figure out how to show it."

"Oh, give me a break," groaned Terri, pulling away from Sonya.

Sonya wagged her head and dragged out her huge makeup bag.

"That bag is big enough to hold a complete disguise for each of us," noted Linda, peering inside.

"I just wanted to be sure we had everything we could possibly need," said Sonya. "I knew the studio was small and there's no makeup person." She pulled out mascaras, eyeliners, eyelash curlers, and various potted creams.

"I think there's enough in there for a lifelong acting career," said Angela.

Dawn sat very still as Sonya applied cream to her face. "I hope none of these cosmetics were tested on animals."

"Yeah, it would be awful to talk about ecology on TV while wearing animal-tested makeup," agreed Linda.

"Don't worry," said Sonya, rubbing cream into Dawn's eyelids. "This makeup is tested on rocks. Pet rocks."

"Oooh, let's make Dawn look a lot older," suggested Angela. "Where is the eye makeup?"

"Don't make me look weird," said Dawn.

"You'll look beautiful," said Sonya. "Now close your eyes."

Dawn closed her eyes and felt a pencil being drawn across her eyelid next to her lashes. Then something was being dusted across her lids.

"Now open your eyes," said Sonya.

"Oooh," exclaimed Angela. "You look pretty."

Sonya applied mascara, then some face makeup. "There. Now look at yourself." She twirled the chair around to face the mirror, which had bright bulbs all around it.

"That's me?" squeaked Dawn in surprise at the unfamiliar, grown-up reflection. She leaned close to the mirror and touched her face. "Gosh, I look so—so adult."

"If we all look as good as you, they'll have to take us seriously," said Angela.

"My turn," said Terri, nudging Dawn out of the chair. "Okay. Plaster it on me, Sonya."

Sonya went to work on Terri, then Angela and Linda. Then Angela did Sonya's face. When they were finished, everyone crowded around the mirror to examine their reflections.

"We look great," whispered Dawn.

"I don't know how anyone will be able to resist us, dahlings," said Angela.

"Let's go show the boys," said Linda.

They trooped out of the dressing room, hands on hips, as if they were models.

"Who are these beautiful girls?" asked Howard, clapping an astonished hand over his mouth.

"I've never seen them before in my life," said Eddie. "Hey, how about a date?"

"Which one of us?" asked Terri.

"All of you," he exclaimed. They all laughed.

"We're going to look awful next to you," said Lyle. "I mean, you girls look so pretty."

"Hey, I've got an idea. Why don't we put makeup on you, too?" asked Sonya.

"Yeah, it's a well-known fact that strong TV lights take all the color out of people's faces," said Linda.

"Permanently?" asked Howard. "Do you mean we might be walking around without color for the rest of our lives because of this experience?"

"Somebody shut him up," said Lyle, socking Howard playfully in the arm.

"Come on. Let's do it," suggested Eddie. "I wanna be gorgeous."

The girls laughed and ushered the boys into a dressing room, where they went to work on them. Ryan was quiet through the entire procedure.

"We don't need to put as much makeup on you guys as we did on ourselves," Sonya explained.

"Why not?" asked Howard.

"We don't suffer such permanent color loss," said Eddie, giggling hysterically.

"Stop that laughing," demanded Angela. "You're wrinkling your makeup!"

"Oh, heavens," quipped Eddie, clapping his hand against his cheek. Angela slapped his hand down.

"Now just stop it," she ordered.

"Yes, ma'am," Eddie said, and the others laughed.

"Gosh, Ryan is cuter than I thought," Terri whispered to Dawn.

"He looks like he has on too much makeup," said Dawn. "It looks weird on boys."

"Yes, but he'll look perfect on TV," said Linda.

Mr. Walinsky came to get them. "Oh, you all look great. Who's the makeup artist?"

Sonya and Angela raised their hands.

"Well done," said Mr. Walinsky. "Now where are your scripts? You know you can't hold them on the set, however."

"I have to read mine just one more time," said Dawn worriedly.

"Loosen up, Dawn. You've been on TV before, remember? You're a celebrity," said Linda, patting her shoulder.

"I know, but I didn't have to memorize anything for that show," Dawn replied. She had once been on a game show called "Family Fortune" with her entire family.

The seats on the set were arranged in a horseshoe shape, with the commentator, Bill Settle, on one end. Mr. Walinsky sat across from him on the other end, and the students sat in the middle chairs.

Everyone quickly took a seat. Dawn was the last in the room, so she took the only remaining chair, which was in the very center, directly facing the small studio audience. She would have much preferred to be sitting behind someone large so that no one could see her.

Mr. Settle introduced the program. "Welcome to our presentation today on 'Hot Stuff,' our cable TV program about and for young people. Today we'll be talking with Mr. Walinsky and some of his students from Banner Junior High. This special group of students are members of the Save a Tree Club, which came into being because of Earth Month.''

Mr. Walinsky then introduced them. Each student smiled when his or her name was called. ''We wanted to do something to contribute to Earth Month at Banner Junior High School,'' Mr. Walinsky said. ''We're lucky enough to have a number of students who are concerned about our environment and who want to make a difference. The young people of today are the adults of tomorrow, and this is the only world they have to inherit. Now I'll ask them to share some important information on how to save energy, to recycle, and how to save our forests and wildlife. Howard, let's start with you.''

Howard smiled. ''Most people don't know this, but if you recycled all the paper bags, newspapers, and other paper waste in your household, you could save two trees a year.''

''Old newspapers can be turned back into pulp, then reprocessed into clean new newspapers,'' said Lyle.

''Ground-up glass can be used in road-building materials,'' said Angela.

''And if you recycle soda cans, you can save the energy it takes to produce new cans,'' added Linda, smiling. ''The cans can be used over again.''

The camera was now on Dawn. She gulped. She felt her face grow hot and red as a sun-ripened tomato. What were her lines?

''Christmas trees,'' Ryan whispered to her.

She cleared her throat. ''You can use plastic Christmas trees instead of cutting down real ones.''

''Plastic isn't biodegradable,'' whispered Angela on her other side.

"Oh, excuse me, I need to add something. Ask for a biodegradable plastic Christmas tree," added Dawn.

"When you shop at the grocery store, ask for paper or biodegradable plastic shopping bags," said Terri.

"And use nonaerosol spray cans instead of aerosol ones," said Ryan so quietly that Mr. Settle had to ask him to repeat himself. Ryan turned very red and beads of sweat stood out on his forehead. His makeup ran in little beige streams down his face.

Dawn felt sorry for him because she understood what it was like to be totally embarrassed.

Angela nudged her suddenly. It was her turn again! "Don't use disposable diapers," said Dawn in a rush. "Did you know disposable diapers account for two percent of the waste in our garbage dumps? Disposable diapers won't decompose for five hundred years."

"Which is a long time for a product that is sometimes used for only fifteen minutes," added Terri.

"If you don't want to wash dirty diapers, use a diaper service," added Dawn.

"Or don't have a baby," added Howard.

"That wasn't in the script," hissed Sonya.

Angela stifled a giggle.

"Plant trees wherever you can because trees clean carbon dioxide from the air and release oxygen back into it. This gives us more oxygen to breathe," said Linda.

"Living things provide one another with substances necessary for life. A proper balance is needed between all living things," said Howard.

"For that reason, we shouldn't be chopping down trees,

clearing huge plots of land, killing plants and animals, and unbalancing our very fragile ecology,'' said Terri.

"That means that we should not be wasteful. When we see pop-tops from soda cans lying on the street, we should pick them up and think of something useful to do with them,'' said Howard. "Otherwise, someone could step on one and get 'toe-maine' poisoning, or—''

Everyone except Mr. Walinsky laughed at the pun.

"Uh, Howard, I don't think that's quite accurate,'' Mr. Walinsky interjected. "Ptomaine poisoning comes from food, I believe.''

"He isn't supposed to be going on and on,'' whispered Dawn, looking around. Mr. Settle was frantically pointing at his watch.

"Yes, sorry, I made a mistake. Ptomaine is a food poisoning. Anyway, a good thing to do with pop-tops is this.'' Slowly Howard removed something from his pants pocket that kept getting hooked onto the fabric. He held it up for all to see. It was an interlocking, looped chain of pop-tops. He went over to Sonya. "Make a necklace for your girlfriend. She'll love you for it, and so will your environment!''

With that, he dropped the necklace carefully over Sonya's head. She blushed, and the entire club and studio audience began clapping.

Dawn could even hear applause coming from backstage.

Mr. Settle stepped forward with his microphone and spoke to the studio audience. "Thank you, Howard, and thank you Mr. Walinsky and the Save a Tree Club from Banner Junior High School, for saving our environment right here in beautiful Gladstone, California—''

Angela developed such a bad case of the giggles that she

collapsed in Dawn's lap. At the same time, Angela's weight was causing Dawn's chair to tip.

"Angela, stop! I'm falling—right off my chair, in front of everyone!" she whispered. Frantically, she pushed on Angela, trying to get her upright. Just at that moment the camera panned over their bright red faces. Dawn thought she would surely die of embarrassment.

Chapter Seven

"Thirteen flat!" shouted Mr. Mitchell. "Dawn, that was fabulous!"

"Really?" she gasped between breaths. "The hundred-meter dash in thirteen flat. Wow! Did you hear that, Terri?"

Terri managed a smile. "Yeah, I heard. It's great," she replied shortly. She had run the distance in thirteen-five.

Coach Mitchell patted Dawn's shoulder. "I think you're our best bet for the hundred-meter dash in the meet, Dawn."

"I thought I was going to be your best bet," said Terri.

Dawn swallowed hard. Of course, Terri would think that. She was the best at every sport she went out for.

"Dawn is a faster sprinter than you are, Terri," explained the coach. "We'll be able to use you for longer races."

"Look, Terri. Longer races are more important than short races anyway," Dawn said quickly.

"Well, they're not more important," corrected the coach. "But fewer people are capable of running a four-hundred-meter dash." Coach Mitchell left the girls to their discussion and went off to work with other kids.

"Yeah. And I can't run fast all the time like you can,"

said Dawn. "I run out of energy. Look, most of the time I can't keep up with you when we ride bikes."

"That's different. You don't even try to ride faster than me," Terri replied grumpily.

Coach Mitchell called Terri over to run the four-hundred-meter dash. Terri took her position and ran around the track at top speed. Dawn watched in awe. The coach was impressed with her time.

"You'll have to practice running longer distances, but you did well for a first time," he told her.

"Goody!" cried Dawn, hugging Terri.

When practice was over, Terri and Dawn rode their bikes to the mall. Linda, Angela, Sonya, Jennifer, and Monique were waiting for them at Sundaze.

"It sure took you long enough to get here," teased Angela.

"Yeah, aren't you supposed to be the fastest girls in town?" said Monique.

"Dawn's the fastest," said Terri, thumping down on one of the pink- and white-striped stools.

"Oh, really?" asked Jennifer with interest.

"That's not true," Dawn said. "Terri is training to run longer races because she can do it. Because I'm short, the coach can only use me for the hundred."

"What was your time, Dawn?" asked Linda.

"Uh, thirteen seconds," she replied, noticing that Terri had looked away.

"Whew! That is fast!" Linda said, whistling through her teeth. "No wonder the coach is excited about you."

"Just call her 'Dynamite Dawn,' " said Terri, and added her order to the list of sundaes.

Dawn sighed. " 'Dynamite Dawn.' I like the sound of that."

Terri wouldn't look at her friend.

"Well, you've been known as 'Terrific Terri' for quite a while now," said Monique. Terri was her idol.

"Yes, after being known as 'Terrible Terri,' " Angela reminded her.

"I don't ever want to hear that again," said Terri darkly.

When the sundaes arrived, Terri ate half of hers, then stabbed her spoon into the rest of it. Dawn noticed she had been unusually quiet since track practice.

"I'm leaving. I want to throw a few hoops," she told the others.

"Hey, wait for us!" cried Dawn.

"No. I want to go right now," said Terri, jumping off her stool. She paid and left the mall.

"What's wrong with her?" asked Dawn.

"She's jealous," said Linda. "She can't stand the idea of you being good at something that she's good at."

"But that's not fair," Dawn said. "I can't help it if I'm good at track, too!"

"Terri takes these things personally," explained Angela.

"She's too competitive," added Sonya.

"It's okay for her to be competitive, but she just can't stand anyone else winning," said Linda.

"That's a problem, especially when the someone else is a best friend," said Dawn.

"I'm worried about her," said Monique.

"Let's go and find her," suggested Jennifer. They finished their sundaes and left the mall.

They found Terri in front of her house, shooting baskets by herself.

Sonya trooped up to her. "Listen, Terri, you can't be the best at everything."

"Why not?" asked Terri, not turning to her at all. She tossed the ball at the basket and it went in.

"Good shot," said Dawn.

"Yeah, why not, Sonya?" asked Monique.

"Because there's always going to be someone better than you at something," said Angela.

"Not if I can help it," replied Terri, moving in for a lay-up.

"Look, isn't it nice that one of your best friends is the one who's better than you rather than a stranger?" asked Jennifer.

"Or Celia Forester?" suggested Sonya.

"At least you could be happy for Dawn," Linda pointed out. "Don't you want her to be successful?"

"Sure I do," said Terri, looking vaguely uncomfortable. She bounced the ball in front of her.

Dawn took the ball and dribbled it, then purposely tripped on a crack in the cement and fell flat on her face. "See? I can't play this stupid game. That's why you signed me up for track, remember?"

"Yeah, I remember," said Terri.

"Well, that settles it," Sonya said. "There's nothing for you to be upset about."

"Do you want to play?" asked Terri, indicating the ball.

"Sure," the others replied.

They started playing, everyone against Terri. Only Linda succeeded in getting the ball from her, and when she did, she dribbled in a wide arc away from Terri and took a jump shot.

Dawn was quick and light on her feet, but she got tired of chasing Terri and Linda around the driveway. Plus, she was tried of not being able to make a basket.

Terri zoomed around the court, dribbling with one hand, then the other, dodging all of them expertly. When she made a basket, Sonya got the rebound. But Terri quickly stole it back and made another basket, then another.

The other girls finally gave up and just stood back to watch Terri make basket after basket.

"Terri, I don't know why you're worried about me," Dawn said. "Everyone knows you're the star athlete."

"Yeah. Everyone knows that," Monique echoed.

Terri grinned. Maybe everything would be okay after all, Dawn thought hopefully.

Chapter Eight

⚘

"Dawn, you'll be Ryan's math partner for this assignment," said Mr. Brent, the math teacher.

Dawn glanced over at Ryan and smiled. Then she looked at Terri across the room. Terri glanced back. Oh, no, thought Dawn.

"Uh, Mr. Brent, could I be partners with Terri?" asked Dawn.

"No, it's all arranged," said Mr. Brent, going on to the next twosome.

Terri was paired with Howard. They were studying simple equations. Dawn had trouble keeping her mind on what they were doing because she was so worried about Terri.

"I enjoyed the tree-planting expedition," Ryan said while they stared at the assignment in their math book.

"Me, too. But I think we're supposed to be concentrating on this assignment," said Dawn. Every so often she glanced over at Terri and found her glaring back at her.

"Oh, yeah, right. Let's see, seventy minus x equals twenty-seven . . ." Ryan read aloud.

Dawn couldn't wait for the class to be over. She tried to

stay as far away from Ryan as she could. But he was sitting right beside her, his hand next to hers on the textbook.

When class was over, she snapped her book shut, nearly catching Ryan's fingers in it.

"You're in a big hurry," he said.

"Sorry. I didn't mean to do that," Dawn replied, gathering up her things.

Terri met her outside class. "Okay, what did he say?"

"Let's see . . . 'x plus one equals y,' and a few other things," replied Dawn.

"Ha-ha. Very funny. I mean anything interesting about himself," persisted Terri, slowing her gait to match Dawn's.

"He said he enjoyed planting trees with us," she said. "We weren't supposed to discuss anything other than math."

"He probably likes you," said Terri, stalking off.

Dawn felt terrible.

At lunch all the girls except Terri were sitting at their regular table in the cafeteria.

"I wish Ryan would stop talking to me and start talking to Terri," said Dawn as she unwrapped her tuna fish sandwich. "It would make my life a whole lot easier."

"He likes you," said Angela.

"I don't want him to," Dawn said with her mouth full. "I might have to do what my sister Mariel does when she doesn't want a guy to be interested in her."

"Like what?" asked Angela.

"Like, sticking her fingers up her nose or pretending to throw up on his shoes," Dawn explained.

The girls laughed.

"Do you really want to go that far, Dawn?" asked Sonya.

"No. Actually, I think it's gross," she replied. "I'd probably just make myself sick if I tried it."

Terri came over to her friends at that moment, her tray full of food. She sat down across from Dawn.

"What're you talking about?" she wanted to know.

"You and Ryan," said Angela. "The romance of the century."

"Give me a break. The guy won't talk to me," she said, crunching down on a taco.

"Maybe you scare him, Terri," suggested Sonya.

"Yeah, you're not the easiest person to talk to," Linda said.

"I don't see why," Terri said. "I don't bite or anything."

"Sometimes you sound like you might," said Angela.

"Well, I don't understand why Ryan will talk to Dawn but not to me," said Terri.

"Dawn doesn't scare anyone," Linda pointed out.

"I am pretty easy to talk to," said Dawn.

Terri just scowled. "Ha. Well, I'm not King Kong."

"Or Godzilla," added Dawn. They laughed.

The after-school track practice found Terri and Dawn running together in the 400-meter relay. Dawn was now running the hundred-meter distance in thirteen.

"I think we might use you as our anchorperson," said Coach Mitchell.

"That's my position," complained Terri.

"We can use you as anchor in the eight-hundred," said the coach. "We need you there."

Terri crossed her arms over her chest. "I won't do it."

"What?" cried Dawn before she could stop herself.

"Terri, this is important," said the coach. "Think of the team, not just yourself."

"You said I'd be the anchor in the four-hundred-meter, and that's what I want to be," she insisted.

"But we need you. You have much more stamina than the other runners, and we need your strength for all the longer races," Coach Mitchell said.

"Find someone else. I know I'm not the only one who can do it," Terri said, staring pointedly at Dawn.

"Terri, we are not going to win our meet without you," said Coach Mitchell.

"That's tough. Count me out," said Terri. She whirled around and stomped off.

"Terri, wait!" cried Dawn, running after her. "Look, I'll give up being the anchor for you! It's not that big a deal to me. I can do hurdles or something."

"No, the coach wants you, not me," said Terri fiercely.

"But he wants you for the more important race!" Dawn persisted. "I don't know why you're so upset!"

"Then you must really be dumb," said Terri.

"Terri, you're not being fair!" Dawn said, still hurrying along beside her.

Terri stopped and faced her. "I'm not? You've taken my position away in the relay, and you're the best bet for the hundred-meter dash, which I thought I had a shot at before. You think I'm not being fair. Right?"

"Look, you can run all the races. I don't want to anymore. Our friendship is more important to me than any stupid old race." Dawn felt tears pricking her eyes and she fought to keep from crying.

Terri started running. Dawn wondered if she should quit

track so Terri could be the winner of all the races. After all, she hadn't wanted to go out for track in the first place. It had been Terri's idea. But now she wanted Terri's friendship back, the way it was before. Nothing in the world seemed as important to her.

Altogether the track team practiced for two and a half weeks before the track meet. Dawn and Terri, who had rejoined the team, were at practice together every day, but Terri refused to say a word to Dawn. Dawn watched Terri run and noted that she made good time. Whenever all the friends got together, Terri would be there, but she wouldn't speak to Dawn.

"This is getting really old, Terri," said Sonya at lunch.

"So? I'll just stop eating lunch with you and talking to you," said Terri stubbornly.

"Are you sure you don't have mules for relatives?" asked Angela.

"My mother would say you're cutting off your nose to spite your face," said Dawn.

"And two wrongs don't make a right," added Linda.

Of course Terri didn't answer. What made matters worse was that Coach Mitchell had decided not to put the two girls in any of the same events. On the day before the track meet, Terri asked that the schedule be changed.

"I want to run in those races," Terri said.

"I don't want you two fighting," said the coach.

"I won't," said Terri. "It's just a race."

The night before the meet, Dawn was terribly nervous. She called all her friends, except Terri, to come over to her house.

"Should I back out of the races?" she asked the group.

"No," said Linda.

"Absolutely not," Angela said fiercely.

"But Terri won't speak to me if I win," she said, tears rolling down her face. "I don't want to lose her friendship."

"Look, don't throw the races," said Sonya. "Let Terri figure out what to do if you win."

"It's just as important for you to win as it is for her," said Linda.

"We can help her come to her senses," said Monique.

"But what if she decides not to be my friend anymore?" asked Dawn. "I couldn't stand that."

"And it would ruin our whole gang," added Jennifer.

"But you have to take this chance," advised Linda. "We have to figure out a way for both of you to be winners."

"Terri still insists she won't run the four-hundred-yard dash or the mile race?" asked Monique.

Dawn nodded.

"Well, why don't we just sign her up," suggested Jennifer with a wink.

"Good idea," said Angela.

"She'll win—I just know it," said Dawn.

Dawn and her friends went to speak to the coach early the morning of the meet—before school began.

"I think it's a great idea," said the coach. "I was thinking of doing it myself. I'll sign her up for everything I would want her to run in. Plus, I'll put her back in the short races with Dawn. That should make her happy."

The field looked fresh and inviting. Runners from three schools wearing numbered tank tops were warming up everywhere. Banner team colors were purple and gold. Dawn was number three. She looked up from her stretching exercises to see her friends in the bleachers, sitting with Howard, Eddie, Lyle, and Ryan. They all gave her the thumbs-up sign, and she did the same.

Terri stomped over to the coach with a copy of the schedule in her hand. "Why am I signed up for all these long races?"

"Because I decided I needed you to run them," replied Coach Mitchell.

"I haven't trained for them, and I'm not going to run them. Period," she said.

"I think you can do it without practice, Terri," said the coach. "I have faith in you."

"I'm not doing it," she said again, striding toward Dawn. "Did you suggest to Mr. Mitchell to sign me up for those races?"

"It wasn't just me. It was all of us," she said, pointing to the bleachers where their friends sat. "We know you can do them all."

"Well, I'm not running those races," Terri insisted.

"Okay, everyone for the hundred-meter dash, please line up over here!" shouted the coach.

Dawn, Terri, and the others lined up.

"Ready, set, go!" cried the starter, someone from one of the other schools. Dawn shot forward, her legs moving like pistons. She heard feet pounding all around her but she didn't know who they belonged to. She heard her friends shouting in the bleachers, "Go, Dawn, go!" Then they yelled, "Go, Terri, terrific Terri—go!" at the top of their lungs. Linda stood up and yelled "Dynamite Dawn!" just as she broke through the finish tape.

Everyone whooped and clapped. After they quieted down,

one of the judges read off the times. "From Banner Junior High, Dawn Selby, thirteen flat; Terri Rivera, thirteen-five; Debbie Bryant, fourteen; Edwards Junior High, Danica Short, thirteen-five; Trisha Evans, fourteen-five; Lydia Collins, fifteen flat. . . . The winner of the hundred-meter dash is Banner Junior High. The winning time is thirteen flat by Dawn Selby."

Her friends stood up and gave her a Dynamite Dawn cheer. Terri gave Dawn a half smile, and managed to throw her a thumbs-up sign.

"Good race, kid," she said.

Next were the relays. Dawn was in anchor position while Terri was next to the last. The race began, with Holly making good time at the beginning, Debbie passing the baton to Terri. Terri snapped up the baton and ran wildly toward Dawn. The baton stung her hand as Terri smacked it into her palm. Dawn ran the rest of the distance as though she were weightless. She felt as if she were flying.

After each team had participated, the judge read out the team times and the split times for each participant. "For Banner Junior High, we have Holly Weisenberg at fifteen flat, Debbie Bryant at fourteen-five, Terri Rivera with fourteen flat, Dawn Selby at thirteen-five, giving Banner a total time of fifty-seven seconds, which makes them the winners of the four-hundred-meter relay!"

When the points for all the events were totaled up, Banner came out on top with thirty-three points to Edwards' twenty and Brentwood's seventeen. The judge handed out ribbons for the various events. Dawn received a blue first-place ribbon for the hundred-meter dash, and each member of the relay team received a blue ribbon for their team's victory. A small gold team trophy was handed to Holly for the four-hundred-meter relay.

"Isn't that great, Terri? We won!" cried Dawn excitedly after it was all over. Two blue ribbons fluttered from her sweaty shirt.

"Yeah, just great," muttered Terri, looking down at her single blue ribbon for the relay and a white third-place ribbon for hurdles.

The friends clambered down the bleachers and rushed out to the field to congratulate Dawn and Terri. Terri didn't wait for them. Instead, she stalked off toward the locker rooms.

"She still can't stand the competition?" Linda asked, shaking her head.

Dawn felt she was going to choke on her tears. "Winning is worse than I ever dreamed it would be," she said miserably.

Chapter Nine

On Friday Dawn and her friends were sitting on the floor of the Selby's living room, waiting for the Earth Month segment to begin on TV.

"I wish Terri were here," she said glumly.

"The way she's acting is driving me crazy," declared Angela.

"She won't do anything with us anymore," said Jennifer.

"Every time I call her, she hangs up," said Dawn.

"I miss her," said Monique. "Even when she comes over to my house, she's not the same person."

"Stop talking! It's starting!" cried Angela, jumping to her feet.

The cable TV show began. The camera moved across the girls' faces, settling on the commentator, Bill Settle. Then the camera focused on each speaker. When it was Dawn's turn, she made a face.

"Ewww! I look like Jemima Puddle-duck," she complained.

"You do not," said Sonya. "I look awful."

When the show reached the part where Howard presented

Sonya with the necklace, Angela sighed and collapsed on the couch.

"Sonya, he is so romantic! You're so lucky," she said.

"He has his moments," Sonya agreed, fingering the pop-top necklace she wore all the time now.

"Terri looks good on TV," said Dawn. "I wonder if she's watching this."

"She probably doesn't want to see our faces," said Angela.

"Come on. She's not that crazy," said Monique. "I'll find out if she watched it."

Next came the part where Angela and Dawn nearly fell off their seats giggling. Everyone burst into laughter watching them.

"What a way to end the show," said Angela.

Dawn's mother ordered Chinese takeout food. The girls sat in the backyard, eating. But everyone's spirits were low because Terri wasn't with them.

"We can't go on like this," said Linda.

"We know," said Dawn. But nobody could think of a single thing to do about it.

"I wonder when Terri will arrive," said Dawn.

It was Sunday and the six girls were at the recycling center with Howard, Lyle, Ryan, and Eddie. The boys were jumping on soda cans while the girls separated clear glass bottles from colored ones.

"Who knows?" said Linda. "She may not ever come."

"But she's so enthusiastic about recycling," said Angela, glancing in the direction of Ryan.

"Yeah, I wouldn't think she'd miss this for the world," said Sonya, wiping a strand of brown hair out of her eyes.

"Being stubborn is more important," said Jennifer.

Howard came over. "Hey, you're missing a member of the gang. Where's Rivera?"

"We don't know," replied Sonya.

"We've been wondering that ourselves," said Dawn.

On Monday Terri didn't show up for track practice. Coach Mitchell approached Dawn.

"Dawn, do you have any idea what's happened to Terri? She didn't show up for practice, and she's always so regular," he said.

"I only know she's mad at me," Dawn replied.

"That's no reason to miss track," the coach said. "We need her."

Dawn went home after practice and stared at her two blue ribbons hanging on her wall. Then she stared at a photo of all of her friends in a plastic frame on her dresser. In it, Terri was smiling as she always used to do. Would she ever smile and laugh again? Dawn wondered. Unfortunately, Terri held the world's record for carrying the longest grudge.

Mrs. Selby knocked on the bedroom door.

"Come in," called Dawn.

"Dawn, what in the world is wrong? You're just staring into space," said Mrs. Selby, wrapping an arm around her daughter's thin shoulders.

"Mom, it's Terri. She won't speak to me. She won't do anything with our group anymore. I don't know what to do about it." She blurted out what had happened at the track meet, how she had won and upset Terri.

Mrs. Selby sat down on the bed. "Dawn, look at me. You must go and speak to Terri now. Make her understand how you feel. Terri must learn to deal with competition, even when it comes from a best friend. She should be happy for your success, and you have a right to enjoy your success, too. I think it's wonderful that you won."

"I did, but not anymore," admitted Dawn. "Right now I think it's pretty awful."

"Well, it isn't. I'm very proud of you, and you should be proud of yourself," said her mother.

After her mother left the room, Dawn thought about what she had said. Suddenly she had an idea.

"I'm going to the bakery, Mom!" she called. Then she jumped on her bike and raced down to the store.

Her sister Mariel was working, making cookies in the back. Mariel's newly bleached hair was white-blond and only an inch long all over her head now. She wore big droopy black earrings.

"What're you doing here?" she asked when she saw Dawn.

"Getting some goodies for a friend," Dawn said. She dropped some still-warm cookies into a white paper bag and searched around for brownies, which were among Terri's favorite things. Finally, she had gathered together a good selection.

"Your friend is going to get a stomachache eating all that stuff," warned Mariel.

"No, she won't. She'll control herself because she's also a health-food nut," explained Dawn. Terri was actually a health-food nut only when she felt like being one, which was about forty percent of the time.

Dawn carefully placed the bag in the basket on her bike

and rode over to Terri's house. Terri was in the driveway shooting baskets.

"Hey, Terri!" Dawn called.

Terri ignored her and just kept shooting. Dawn got off her bike and started talking.

"I need to talk to you. You make me feel bad about winning. I'm supposed to feel good about it, but I can't because of you."

"Feel good. That's what you're supposed to do," said Terri gruffly.

"You're good at every sport, and I've just found one that I'm good at," Dawn went on. "Why can't you let me be good at just one thing?"

"I'm not stopping you," Terri said, without facing her. "Knock yourself out."

Dawn put the bag of cookies down. Terri stepped back onto the bag.

"Watch out! I brought you something," Dawn said, whisking the bag into her arms again.

She stared inside the bag, which was now partly crumbs. She felt like throwing the bag at Terri.

"If you were really my friend, Terri, you wouldn't be acting like this," Dawn declared.

Terri shrugged without turning to look at her. Dawn dropped the bag of cookies on the driveway and climbed on her bicycle. As she rode home, tears streamed from her eyes into her hair. She wished that Terri had never signed her up for track in the first place.

Chapter Ten

⚘

"Where are the trees?" asked Dawn as the five girls stood waiting outside the state park ranger's station. It was Tuesday and a school holiday. They were waiting for Mr. Walinsky to arrive so they could go tree planting. Dawn fingered her lucky gold bracelet, which she had worn in the hopes that things would go better that day. But it didn't seem promising, she thought. Terri still stood off to one side, not speaking to anyone.

"I think a ranger dropped the trees off in the woods already," said Linda.

Just then, Mr. Walinsky drove up in his truck with Lyle and Howard next to him on the front seat.

"Where's Ryan?" asked Terri.

"He had to work today," said Howard. "But we're here!"

"The two stooges," Angela muttered under her breath.

"Are you ready for a hike, girls?" Mr. Walinsky asked. "The tree-planting site is about two miles from here."

"I've never been in better shape in my life," declared Dawn, hoisting her backpack onto one shoulder.

"Do we have to?" groaned Angela. "I had a big breakfast."

"This is a great way to walk it off," said Sonya.

Terri charged ahead of the others, leading the way up the trail. Mr. Walinsky came next, walking in front of the boys. Because Angela was feeling slow, Dawn, Sonya, and Linda kept her company at the back of the line.

About an hour later they arrived at the scene. The saplings were lying on the ground, their ball roots wrapped in burlap.

"I'd love to be a tree," Howard said in a singsong while the girls dragged the trees to the clearing where they'd plant them.

"Why don't you help?" asked Terri.

"And I think a tree would love to be me," Howard went on, ignoring her.

Lyle wrapped himself in a branch. "A tree would like to be free like me."

"To walk and run happily," added Howard, hopping onto a tree stump.

"To have eyes so it could see," Lyle said. "But I would like to be a tree so that my branches could move when it's windy."

"And so that I could have roots that grow deeply," said Howard.

"Very good!" exclaimed Angela, clapping.

"I didn't know you were poets," said Sonya.

"They're pains, not poets," said Terri.

"Now can you guys help us dig these holes?" asked Linda in exasperation.

"I thought you were liberated," said Lyle.

"Yeah, you don't need us," said Howard.

Terri frowned at them. "Of course we don't *need* you. But you've got to help."

"Okay. Shovels, please," said Howard. He and Lyle started digging.

"I think we should put a message at the roots of this tree," suggested Dawn. "Then a hundred years from now someone can dig it up and find our message."

"What a good idea," said Angela. "We could write something about ourselves."

"Maybe we should write about what it's like to be in junior high in these times," said Howard.

"We could include our tree poem," said Lyle.

"Let's do it all," said Linda. Each of them wrote a message on a slip of notepaper stating her or his name, age, school, grade, and interests. Lyle and Howard wrote down their poem and placed it in the soda-pop can with the other notes. Then they laid the can in the hole with one of the trees.

When everyone had finished digging, they set the trees in the ground, then shoveled dirt around them and packed it down. After they watered the trees, they were ready to go.

The group made their way down the trail to the ranger station, singing "When Johnny Comes Marching Home Again" as a round. By the time they reached the station, they were laughing and falling all over each other.

They went straight to the canteen to get snacks. Dawn was standing in line behind Sonya and Howard, who were holding hands. Terri was ahead of them all, talking to Mr. Walinsky. Seeing Terri made Dawn reach for her bracelet, hoping for a dose of good luck. It wasn't there! She searched up and down her arm, but it was gone!

"My lucky bracelet! I lost it!" she blurted.

Everyone turned to look at her. Howard and Sonya were holding cardboard trays full of hot dogs and drinks.

"Your what?" asked Angela.

"You know, my lucky bracelet. The one my parents gave me for my last birthday," she explained tearfully.

"Why'd you wear a good bracelet on a hike?" Sonya wanted to know.

"It doesn't matter. It's gone," Dawn said. "I'll have to go back up and look for it."

"I'll go with you," offered Sonya.

"Me, too," said Angela.

"Well, you can't leave me out," said Linda. "Coming, Terri?"

Terri reluctantly agreed. "Tell Mr. Walinsky we went to look for Dawn's bracelet," she told Howard. Mr. Walinsky had just gone to speak with the ranger.

With heads bent low, they went back up the trail, searching every inch. When they reached the planting site, the girls split up and scanned the earth around each tree they had planted. Dawn was retracing her steps when suddenly she saw something shiny lying next to a big tree. She gasped and ran toward it, but her foot got wedged under a giant tree root. She fell flat on her face, her foot still stuck under the root. Just out of her reach, nestled between more tree roots, was the bracelet.

"I found it!" she cried out. "Over here!" She stretched but couldn't quite reach the bracelet. The girls ran over to her.

"That's great. I'm so glad," said Sonya, holding the bracelet up to the light. "The clasp is loose. You'll have to get it fixed. It's so pretty."

Dawn dislodged her foot and tried to stand up. "Uh, can you help me up?"

"You hurt yourself. Where?" asked Sonya.

"My foot got stuck under this tree root and I fell," she explained, rubbing her foot.

Angela and Linda knelt on either side of her and lifted her. "Can you walk on it?" Linda asked.

Dawn tried to put pressure on the foot, and pain shot through it. "No, I don't think so."

"Do you think it's broken?" asked Sonya.

"I don't know. I've never broken any bones before," replied Dawn.

"You see stars when you break a bone," said Terri, coming forward. "Sometimes you feel like you're going to faint."

"That didn't happen," Dawn told her.

"You probably sprained your foot, then," said Angela.

"You do need to see a doctor, though," said Linda.

"We're way out in the middle of nowhere, miles from civilization," declared Angela dramatically. "The rangers won't come by this way for hours probably."

"And Mr. Walinsky doesn't even know we're up here," added Sonya.

"Yes, he does. I told Howard to tell him," Terri said. "But I'm sure they won't come after us right away."

"There are probably wild animals in these woods at night," said Dawn, shivering.

"We're not staying out here past dark!" cried Sonya.

"We could carry Dawn down the trail," suggested Linda.

"No, I'll go for help," Terri offered gruffly.

"But it's so far," Dawn said.

"Not for me," said Terri. "See you guys later." She waved and started running back down the trail.

Chapter Eleven

⚘

"I wonder if Terri's okay," Dawn said as Angela and Linda helped her find a comfortable position at the base of the tree.

"She's probably fine. You know how tough she is," said Sonya.

"Yeah, but her feelings get hurt so easily," Dawn pointed out. "I'm just afraid she's still so mad at me that . . ." She didn't want to finish her thoughts aloud—that maybe Terri was so mad at her that she wouldn't come back. Terri might be glad she had hurt her foot because that would mean she wouldn't be able to race against her!

As if she knew what Dawn was thinking, Linda said, "It doesn't matter how angry Terri is, Dawn, she's still one of us."

"Yeah, she's a best friend," said Sonya.

"She'll do what's right for you in the end," added Angela.

"I hope so. You know, I wore my lucky bracelet today because I hoped Terri and I would be able to make up. But so far it's only brought me bad luck!" cried Dawn. "First I lost the bracelet, then I found it with its clasp broken, and then I hurt my foot."

"At least you found it," said Linda.

"And you only hurt your foot," said Angela. "You're not dead."

"Right. It's not the worst thing that could happen," said Sonya.

An hour crawled by. Terry still hadn't returned.

"I wonder if she's coming," Dawn said worriedly.

"Of course she is," said Angela.

Dawn began to doze off to sleep. But she was awakened by the sound of a truck. She opened her eyes to see a state park truck coming toward them—Terri was waving from the truckbed.

"Hooray, they're here!" cried Angela, jumping up.

The truck stopped near Dawn. Terri, Ryan, a ranger, and Mr. Walinsky jumped out and ran over to her. Then two paramedics followed.

"What are you doing here, Ryan?" asked Dawn, surprised to see him. "I thought you were busy today."

"I am. My father's a ranger, and I help as a volunteer for the rescue team here," he explained. "That's why I couldn't plant trees with you guys today."

"Dawn, Terri told me what happened. How do you feel?" asked Mr. Walinsky.

"I'm okay. It just hurts a little," said Dawn. The paramedics examined her foot carefully.

"It looks like a sprain," one of them said. "It probably hurts a lot, but you'll be okay."

"Will she be able to run?" Terri asked.

"Well, not for a couple of weeks, but it will heal," said the paramedic. "We'll have a doctor look at it."

"A couple of weeks!" declared Terri. "What about track?"

"It's okay, Terri," said Dawn. "I can always run after that."

"Yes, but we'll have our next meet in a couple of weeks. You won't be able to practice for it," Terri pointed out.

"I'll be okay," said Dawn.

"You girls should never have come up here without supervision," said Mr. Walinsky.

"We know," Angela, Sonya, Dawn, and Linda chorused.

"Something much more serious could've happened. Then what would we have done?" he said.

"I don't know," said Dawn miserably. "I'm sorry for causing so much trouble."

"It won't happen again, Mr. Walinsky," said Linda.

"I'll make sure it doesn't," said Mr. Walinsky.

The paramedics carried her to the truck and laid her down in the back. Terri sat down beside her. Sonya, Linda, and Angela sat on Dawn's other side. Ryan rode up front with Mr. Walinsky.

"It's my fault you can't run," said Terri suddenly.

"No, it's not," protested Dawn. "I was clumsy."

"I know you were, but if I hadn't been such a jerk, you wouldn't have worn that dumb bracelet," said Terri. "And if you hadn't worn the bracelet, this wouldn't have happened."

Dawn knew that she was right. "How did you know about the bracelet?"

"Because I know you, and you wore it because you hoped we would make up and that everything would be okay," Terri told her.

"You must be a mind reader!" Dawn exclaimed.

Terri shook her head. "You know I don't believe in that

psychic stuff. We've just been friends so long I know how you think.''

"Well, everything went wrong in spite of the bracelet," said Dawn.

"You shouldn't believe in lucky bracelets," Terri told her.

"Maybe not," said Dawn. "But I didn't know what else to do.''

"I'm really sorry, Dawn," said Terri. "I don't know how you can stand to be friends with me.''

"It isn't always easy," admitted Dawn.

"Yeah, you have to be really devoted," said Sonya.

"But you did run down the mountain to get help for me," said Dawn. "Only a real, true friend would do that.''

"No big deal. You would've done the same for me. I really wanted you to be a good runner, Dawn. It's fun to be good at something, and I want you to win," Terri said. "Honest.''

"It sure didn't seem like it before," Angela pointed out.

"Yeah, Terri. You made Dawn feel awful about winning," Linda said.

"I didn't mean to. When I realized what it would be like if I were you, Dawn, winning a race and having my best friend get mad at me for it, I knew I was wrong," Terri said. "I have to be able to take a little competition, especially from my friends.''

Dawn tried to sit up to her full height, and winced. "I'm not just a 'little' competition," she said.

"That's right. She might be small, but on the track, she's tall," quipped Sonya. The girls laughed.

"And what about Ryan?" asked Dawn. "You knew I wasn't interested in boys.''

"I'm sorry about that, too," Terri said. "Now that he's talking to me, I realize how dumb I've been."

"He talks to you?" Dawn asked.

"Well, yeah. He's impressed with me because I ran down the trail to get help for you," Terri explained, grinning.

"My heroine," said Dawn. "Thanks, Terri."

"Hey, no problem," Terri said.

The truck drove up to the ranger station and the paramedics transferred Dawn to Mr. Walinsky's truck. Everyone piled in and the advisor drove the short distance to the hospital. Ryan came with them.

They waited in the emergency room for a doctor to see Dawn. Mr. Selby burst in the door, looking worried.

"Where's my baby?" he asked.

"Over here!" cried the girls, pointing at Dawn. He came over and hugged his daughter.

"I didn't recognize you with your foot as big as it is," he said jokingly. Dawn's foot had grown to almost twice its normal size. "How do you feel?"

"Okay. Just don't ask me to walk, and I'll feel fine," she said.

"I guess this means the end of your track career," he said.

"No, it doesn't, Dad," Dawn insisted. "I'll be fine in time for the next meet!"

"That's right, Mr. Selby," said Terri, slapping Dawn on the shoulder. "She's our star."

"I can't believe Terri ran two miles to the ranger station to get help for you, Dawn," Ryan said.

"Ryan runs in marathons, but not at school," Terri added.

"Why not?" asked Dawn.

He shrugged and blushed. "I just like to run alone, I guess.

And I like long distances. I was telling Terri she should run long distances.''

"I'm going to be running in the mile race for the city. It was Ryan's idea," Terri said. "And just for fun, next week we're going to run against each other.''

Dawn exchanged glances with her friends. "Can you handle it, Terri?"

"Sure, no problem," Terri said, grinning.

Dawn and her friends burst out laughing as Dawn was wheeled into an examining room.

Chapter Twelve

⌘

"I can't stand watching you run when I can't," Dawn said to Terri after track practice. She sat in the bleachers. On her sprained foot she wore an Ace bandage and had to walk with crutches that she'd need for another week.

Terri wiped sweat from her forehead with a white towel. "You'll catch up with me soon enough."

Angela, Sonya, Linda, Monique, and Jennifer were all sitting with Dawn.

"Remember, Dawn, that a few weeks ago you didn't even like track," said Monique.

"Terri had to sign you up secretly," Sonya added.

"Yeah. And a few weeks ago, you guys didn't know a thing about planting trees," Dawn reminded them.

"Or recycling," added Angela.

"Or fighting developers," said Sonya. She pulled a crumpled letter out of her pocket. "Which reminds me. We received a letter from our city planning commission."

The girls squashed close together so they could read over Sonya's shoulder.

Dear Save a Tree Club:

Thank you for your recent letter telling us about the developers. We are pleased to find students in the community who are interested in protecting our environment. Therefore, we would like to extend to you an invitation to attend our next planning-commission meeting on Tuesday.

You can be part of the decision-making process. Usually, land such as you describe has to be rezoned for building in forest areas, and we are the ones who decide whether to rezone or not. We look forward to seeing you there.

> Dorothy Bidwell,
> Gladstone City Planning Commission

"Oh, goody," said Dawn. "They're taking us seriously."

"They may change their minds after they see us," said Terri.

"I hope they didn't see our TV show," said Angela. "We were so embarrassing."

"Well, I'm wearing my lucky bracelet to the meeting, just in case," said Dawn.

"I thought you said it didn't work," said Terri.

"You weren't going to believe in lucky bracelets anymore," Linda pointed out.

"I wasn't, but then Terri and I got back together," said Dawn, beaming. "And now I believe in it again. It made my dream come true."

Terri grinned.

Runners filed off the track toward the locker room. The

girls helped Dawn stand up and get organized with her crutches.

"I didn't know they made crutches for midgets," teased Terri.

"They call them stilts," said Dawn.

"Terri, time me, please!" cried Monique.

"If you insist," said Terri. She took off her sports watch and stood next to the now empty track. Monique inched her sneaker up to the chalk starting line. "Okay, ready, set, go!"

Monique took off, her skinny legs moving so fast they blurred. When she was finished, Terri glanced down at her watch.

"Well?" said Dawn.

"Yeah, how'd I do?" insisted Monique, wiping her sweaty forehead with the back of her hand.

"You're amazing," Terri said. "You ran the hundred-meter dash in fourteen. And you've never even tried before."

"Wow! I can't wait to go to junior high!" exclaimed Monique, flinging her arms around Terri.

"I think we're looking at the next junior-high track star," said Dawn.

"Just think, if I practice running now, I could be fabulous by next year," Monique went on excitedly.

"Today, Banner Junior High. Tomorrow, the Olympics," said Sonya.

"Hey, Monique. Go for it," said Dawn, grinning. "Terri has trained some of the best runners." She made a motion with her fist as though she were polishing a medal on her chest.

"And it's only her first track season," Linda pointed out.

"Already she's a phenomenal success!" quipped Angela.

"Oh, Monique, I forgot to tell you. I already signed you up for next year," said Terri.

"What?" Monique gasped. "You didn't! I have to ask my father first!"

Dawn, Terri, and the others exchanged glances, then burst into laughter.

"Just kidding!" they chorused.

About the Author

SUSAN SMITH was born in Great Britain and has lived most of her life in California and New York. She began writing when she was thirteen years old and has authored a number of novels for teenagers, including the *Samantha Slade* series by Archway Paperbacks. She is married and lives in Santa Fe, New Mexico, with her three children. The children have provided her with many ideas and observations that she has included in her books. In addition to writing, Ms. Smith enjoys travel, horseback riding, skiing, and swimming.

Look for Best Friends #13:

Who's Out to Get Linda?

coming in April 1991

When Linda runs for president of the seventh-grade class, she believes she's left her past behind her. Then someone sends her anonymous messages threatening to reveal her secrets. The Best Friends think it's Celia, their old enemy, who is also running for class president. Could this be another of her pranks? When some undercover work in the girls' restroom suggests other possibilities, the girls don't know what to think. Now a message has been left on the blackboard for the entire seventh grade to see. Suddenly Linda has no secrets left. She is so embarrassed she's ready to leave Gladstone forever! Can Linda still win the election? Can the Best Friends stop this mysterious person from ruining Linda's life? Or is it already too late?

WATCH OUT FOR...
Sheila Greenwald

Sheila Greenwald brings you more
fun and excitement with the
hilarious adventures of her
young heroine Rosy Cole.